THREE BEDTIME STORIES

THE THREE BEARS
THE THREE LITTLE KITTENS
THE THREE LITTLE PIGS
PICTURES BY GARTH WILLIAMS

A GOLDEN BOOK, NEW YORK
Western Publishing Company, Inc., Racine, Wisconsin 53404

The Three Bears

ONCE upon a time there were three bears—a great big father bear, a middle-sized mother bear, and a little baby bear.

They lived in a little house in the forest.

And every morning those three bears went for a walk while their porridge cooled for breakfast.

One day a little girl, who was called Goldilocks because of her golden curls, went for a walk in the forest.

And she came to the house of the three bears.

Knock knock knock at the door went Goldilocks. But of course there was no answer. For the three bears were out for their walk.

So Goldilocks went into the house.

She saw three chairs. She sat in Father Bear's great big chair. It was much too hard.

She sat in Mother Bear's middle-sized chair. It was much too soft.

She sat in Baby Bear's little chair. It was just right! But the little chair broke in two!

"How hungry I am!" said Goldilocks when she
saw the three bowls of porridge.

She tasted the porridge in Father Bear's great
big bowl. It was much too hot.

She tasted the porridge in Mother Bear's middle-
sized bowl. It was much too cold.

She tasted the porridge in Baby Bear's little
bowl. It was just right! And Goldilocks ate it all up.

Then up the stairs went Goldilocks to take a nap.

She tried Father Bear's great big bed. It was much too hard.

She tried Mother Bear's middle-sized bed. It was much too soft.

She tried Baby Bear's little bed. It was just right! Goldilocks lay down in it and fell fast asleep.

Then home came the three bears.

"Someone has been sitting in my chair!" said Father Bear in a great big voice.

"And someone has been sitting in my chair!" said Mother Bear, in a middle-sized voice.

"Someone has been sitting in my chair!" said Baby Bear in a little baby voice. "And now my chair is broken!"

"Someone has been tasting my porridge!" said Father Bear in a great big voice.

"And someone has been tasting my porridge!" said Mother Bear in a middle-sized voice.

"Someone has been tasting my porridge!" said Baby Bear in a little baby voice. "And someone has eaten it all up!"

Then up the stairs they went.

"Someone has been lying in my bed!" said Father Bear in a great big voice.

"And someone has been lying in my bed!" said Mother Bear in a middle-sized voice.

"Someone has been lying in my bed!" said Baby Bear in a little baby voice. "Someone is still there!"

Then Goldilocks woke up and saw the three bears. She got such a fright that she jumped right up and ran down the stairs, out of the house, and into the forest. And Goldilocks never went back to that little house again!

The Three Little Kittens

The three little kittens,
They lost their mittens,
And they began to cry,
"Oh Mother dear,
We sadly fear
Our mittens we have lost!"

"What! lost your mittens,
You naughty kittens?
Then you shall have no pie."
"Meow, meow, meow!"

The three little kittens,
They found their mittens,
And they began to cry,
"Oh Mother dear,
See here, see here,
Our mittens we have found!"

"What! found your mittens,
You good little kittens?
Then you shall have some pie."
"Purr, purr, purr."
The three little kittens
Put on their mittens,
And soon ate up the pie.

"Oh Mother dear,
We greatly fear
Our mittens we have soiled!"
"What! soiled your mittens,
You naughty kittens?"
Then they began to sigh,
"Meow, meow, meow!"

The three little kittens,
They washed their mittens,
And hung them up to dry.
"Oh Mother dear,
Look here, look here,
Our mittens we have washed!"

"What! washed your mittens?
You darling kittens!
But I smell a rat close by!
Hush, hush, hush!"
"Meow, meow, meow!"

The Three Little Pigs

ONCE upon a time three little pigs went out into the world to seek their fortunes.

Now the first thing each of them had to do was build a house to live in.

The first little pig met a man carrying a bundle of straw.

"Please sir," he said, "give me some straw to build myself a house."

The straw house was quickly built, and the little pig was just settling down nicely when a big bad wolf knocked at the door and said,

"Little pig, little pig, let me come in!"

"Not by the hair on my chinny chin chin!" said the first little pig.

Then the big bad wolf huffed and he puffed, and he blew the house in.

He ate up the fat little pig. And that was the end of the first little pig.

The second little pig built himself a house of
sticks. He was just putting the finishing touches
to the window curtains when the big bad wolf
knocked at the door and said,

"Little pig, little pig, let me come in!"

"Not by the hair on my chinny chin chin!" said
the second little pig.

Then the big bad wolf huffed and he puffed, and he puffed and he huffed, and he blew the house in.

He ate up the second little pig. And that was the end of *that* little pig.

Now the third little pig had built himself a house of bricks. It took him much longer to build than a straw house, or a house of sticks.

The little pig had just got the last brick in place when the big bad wolf knocked at the door and said,

"Little pig, little pig, let me come in!"

"Not by the hair on my chinny chin chin!" said the third little pig.

Then the big bad wolf huffed and he puffed,
and he puffed and he huffed.

But he could not blow the house in!

The little brick house stayed there, with the fat
little pig safe inside it.

"It's no good hiding, little pig," said the wolf.
"I shall come down the chimney."

"Come ahead!" said the little pig. And he put a big pot of water on the fire to boil.

The big bad wolf came down the chimney and landed right in the pot of boiling water.

The third little pig had wolf stew for dinner that night.

And *that* was the end of the big bad wolf.